Alison Lohans
SUNDOG RESCUE

Vladyana Langer Krykorka

Annick Press Ltd.
Toronto • New York • Vancouver

THE CANADA COUNCIL | LE CONSEIL DES ARTS
FOR THE ARTS | DU CANADA
SINCE 1957 | DEPUIS 1957

We acknowledge the support of the Canada
Council for the Arts for our publishing program.
We also thank the Ontario Arts Council.

Cataloguing in Publication Data

Lohans, Alison, 1949-
  Sundog rescue

ISBN 1-55037-571-7 (bound) ISBN 1-55037-570-9 (pbk.)

I. Krykorka, Vladyana. II. Title.

PS8573.O35S96 1999   jC813'.54   C98-932766-3
PZ7.L65Su 1999

The art in this book was rendered in watercolors and colored pencils.
The text was typeset in Trumpet Lite.

Distributed in Canada by:
Firefly Books Ltd.
3680 Victoria Park Avenue
Willowdale, ON
M2H 3K1

Published in the U.S.A. by Annick Press (U.S.) Ltd.
Distributed in the U.S.A. by:
Firefly Books (U.S.) Inc.
P.O. Box 1338, Ellicott Station
Buffalo, NY 14205

Printed and bound in Canada by
Friesens, Altona, Manitoba.

For my mother, Mildred Lohans, and for Muriel Neithercut
and Myrna Guymer, who are all wonderful grandmas.

–A.L.

In memory of my mother, Anna Langer Vanek, who created
all the beautiful needlework in this book.

–V.L.K.

$\mathcal{S}$ometimes Melissa saw things that nobody else did.

"Y ou're weird," her brother Adam said when Melissa worried about the puddle-sharks that bit people's boots.

Wiggling cold toes in wet socks, Melissa went inside and told her grandma.

Grandma gave her a hug. "I used to see things, too," she said. Then Grandma told Melissa about the bearded face up in the hayloft in the barn, when she was a little girl.

"Tell me about the olden days," said Melissa.

So Grandma told about riding to school in a sleigh. Grandma's mama used to bundle Grandma and her sisters in furry robes, and put toasty-hot bricks from the oven by their feet. "The cold seemed so big and lonely," Grandma said. "Some days I feared it might even swallow me up."

When it was time for Grandma to go home, Melissa's toes weren't cold anymore.

hen Melissa told her dad about the big-eared mice that lived in the caragana hedge, he said, "There's nothing there." And he ruffled Melissa's hair. Adam looked too, but all he found was an old tennis ball. Probably the mice were hiding.

On hot summer days Melissa could see them creeping around in the shade, nibbling weeds and scaring away birds that came too close. They scared Melissa, too.

on't worry," Grandma whispered. "They'll go away, sooner or later." Then she told Melissa about the small feathered fox that lurked outside the henhouse when she was a little girl. Mama and Papa were often too busy to listen. But Granny Babi used to rock little-girl-Grandma by the wood stove and help her smile her fears away.

When a rock bounced up from a passing truck and hit the windshield, only Melissa saw the spiderlegs wriggling in the shiny new chip in the glass. She wondered if Grandma might have seen them, too. But Grandma wasn't there.

elissa laughed when she saw tiny ice-people scampering across the frosty lawn. She set down the paper snowflake she was making, and ran to tell Grandma. Grandma told Melissa about the magic eyelash screen. "When I was little," she said, "my Granny Babi showed me this." Together, they squinched their eyelashes just right and saw beautiful sparkly colors. The ice-people turned into butterflies, and then they were gone.

One very cold winter day when Adam and Dad were at a hockey tournament and Mom had a lot of work to do, Melissa stayed with Grandma. Melissa cut picture-people out of old magazines, and built towers with Grandma's spools of thread. They baked gingersnaps, and traced their fingers on frost-feathers on the windowpane. Grandma told stories about the olden days.

In the summer Grandma and her sisters used to splash in the pond. With their dresses on! One time in the winter, Grandma stayed too late visiting the new baby at the next farm. "I was walking home all by myself," she said, "and it got so dark I had no idea which way to turn. Finally I heard sleigh bells, and my papa calling. Then I knew I was safe."

When it was time for Melissa to go home, Grandma's car groaned and wouldn't go. The cold reached for Melissa and Grandma with long white fingers; it shivered their eyeballs and crept in through their noses.

Grandma called Melissa's mom but the line was busy. Six gingersnaps later it was still busy.

We'll walk," said Grandma. She bundled Melissa up until she felt stiff and fat as a snowgirl. Grandma bundled up too, until all that showed were two blue eyes in a stripe of face. "When I was little," said Grandma, "on days like this you could almost hear sunlight dancing; somehow it eased the bitter cold."

"I wish we could ride home in a sleigh," Melissa said into her scarf. "With bells. And hot bricks by our feet."

Outside, the sundogs were very bright. "Look!" Melissa said, tugging at Grandma's hand. Grandma's eyes smiled. "Isn't that amazing?" she said. "You'd never think ice crystals could shine just like the sun." Melissa looked at the sundogs until colored spots wobbled in front of her.

In the big, quiet outdoors, frost-flowers bloomed in all the trees. "Chip! Chip!" said fluffy bird-balls in the lilac bushes. Kthweek-kthwokk, kthweek-kthwokk, went Melissa's and Grandma's boots on the squeaky sparkly snow.

They came to the frozen river with Melissa's house on the opposite side. Kthwook-kthwokk, kthwook-kthwokk, went their boots in deeper snow. Kthwook-kthwokk-KTHWUUUUPFF! as Grandma fell down the riverbank.

Grandma lay there and didn't move.

"GRANDMA!" screamed Melissa. Her heart went thump-thump-thump! beneath her bundled-up sweaters and snowsuit; her tummy felt cold and scared.

Grandma's eyes blinked open. "I've hurt my foot," she said. "Melissa, you'll have to run and get your mother."

Melissa looked over her shoulder. She was sure something was hiding in the willows that grew along the riverbank. And there they were, dark fearsome shadow-wolves! "The shadow-wolves will get me!" she cried. "They might eat you, too!"

"Be brave," said Grandma. And Grandma tried to smile. Melissa remembered how Babi used to help Grandma smile her fears away. But Melissa couldn't smile.

elissa looked at her house with smoke puffing from the chimney. Then she took a big deep breath and ran. Swisshhhh! across the green-gray ice. Snap! went the ice, way down deep.

The shadow-wolves were sniffing!

"Keep going, Melissa," Grandma called in a faraway voice. Melissa stumbled up the riverbank, flopping through the deep, deep snow. The shadow-wolves followed close behind. "Go away!" she shouted. But they didn't.

High in the sky the shining sundogs watched.

Then Melissa remembered something. Huffing hard, she squinched her eyes to make the magic eyelash screen.

The sundogs grew and grew. They barked and growled; they snapped and howled. The sundogs scared the wolves away.

elissa ran and got her mom. Kthweek-kthwokk-kthweek-kthwokk-kthweek-kthwokk-kthweek-kthwokk! went their hurrying boots. Thud-thud, swisshhhh! across the ice to Grandma.

"That's my brave girl," Grandma said with chattering teeth as Melissa wrapped a blanket around her. "Babi would be proud of you."

Hugging Grandma, Melissa could feel furry robes keeping them snug. And oven-hot bricks by their feet. Then, kthwokk-kthwokk-kthwokk-kthwokk went their careful boots as Melissa and her mom and Grandma limped home.

Melissa looked over her shoulder.

A shadow-wolf! It was watching! Melissa closed her eyes and tried to smile. When she looked again, the shadow-wolf was fading. It just melted away until it was hard to tell the difference between the wolf and the gray-blue shadows that stretched across the snow.

Melissa squeezed Grandma's hand and listened carefully. She was sure she could hear bells on a sleigh. And just maybe, horses' hooves squunching in the snow.